Mortal Terror

Robert Brustein

A SAMUEL FRENCH ACTING EDITION

SAMUEL FRENCH

FOUNDED 1830

SAMUELFRENCH.COM
SAMUELFRENCH-LONDON.CO.UK

MORTAL TERROR was first produced by the Suffolk Theatre and Boston Playwrights Theatre, at the Modern Theatre, Boston, in 2011. The performance was directed by Daniela Varon, with sets by Jon Savage, costumes by Rachel Padula Shufell, lighting by Frank Meissner, Jr., and s ound by David Remedios. The Production Stage Manager was L. Arkansas Light. The cast was as follows:

SIR JOHN HARINGTON. . . . . Dafydd Ap Rees

WILL SHAKESPEARE. . . . . Stafford Clark-Price

JOHN MARSTON . . . . John Kuntz

BEN JONSON . . . . .Jeremiah Kissel

KING JAMES.. . . . . Michael Hammond

QUEEN ANNE. . . . . Georgia Liman

ROBERT CATESBY. . . . . .Christopher James Webb

GUY FAWKES, ALSO KNOWN AS GUIDO. . . . . John Kuntz

CHARACTERS

WILL SHAKESPEARE – 41, poet and playwright

JOHN MARSTON – 29, satirist and playwright

BEN JONSON – 33, poet and playwright

SIR JOHN HARINGTON – 44, courtier and poet

KING JAMES I OF ENGLAND – 39, author of *Daemonologie*

ANNE OF DENMARK – 31

ROBERT CATESBY – 39, a Catholic nobleman, 39

GUY FAWKES – 35, a terrorist

*(The action moves freely from place to place so the scenery should be spare, suggestive, versatile. The time is 1605 — just two years after a recurrence of the fearsome bubonic pestilence called The Black Death which had hit London once again, this time taking 33,000 lives. We are in a room in Cripplegate, **SHAKESPEARE**'s digs during the year of these happenings. Spartan accommodations. A writing table with quills and ink and pages. The lights come up on **WILL** writing. He is 41, older now by twelve years than in* The English Channel. *Quite elegant and aristocratic as in the newly-discovered Cobbes portrait. His face has kept its good nature, though it is not a stranger to melancholy, expectant of more ill fortune to come.)*

(A thin scarecrow figure dressed all in black bursts into the room, his face muffled with a scarf.)

MARSTON. Will, for the sake of my safety and your salvation, give me sanctuary!

WILL. *(skeptical)* And what muffled stranger is this demands my sanctuary?

MARSTON. *(removing the scarf)* You do not recognize the features of your feckless fellow fabulist, John Marston?

WILL. Marston!

MARSTON. Conceal me for Christ's sake! I'm in mortal terror. That personage is severely demented.

WILL. What "personage" do you mean, man?

MARSTON. Why, him, *him.* The lunatical Ben Jonson.

WILL. Irritable, yes, splenetic perhaps, but rarely lunatical, as you call him.

MARSTON. Hush. No time for further expostulation. I hear his thunderous boots upon the passage stairwell. *(harsh whisper)* HIDE ME!

(sound of heavy boots coming up the stairs)

WILL. In there. And be still! (**WILL** *pushes* **MARSTON** *offstage as if into a cupboard)*

(Enter **BEN JONSON,** *red-faced and breathless, carrying a whip. At this time,* **BEN** *is about thirty-three, but already seems physically middle-aged. He is heavy and bulbous-nosed and deliberate in his movements.)*

BEN. Where is that constipated little poetaster? I'll be damned if I didn't see his blotchy backside bobbing up your stairs!

WILL. Calm, Ben. You are as rigid as a fence pole.

BEN. I'll squash that noxious piece of vermin like a horse fly. Marston's here, I know it! You can smell his farts whenever he's in panic. Who else expresses fear in such a glandular manner?

WILL. Tush! The man is but a harmless little scribbler.

BEN. With the cheek to insult his betters from the public stage.

WILL. He insulted you?

BEN. Through the mouth of one of his crapulous characters.

WILL. I would have accepted that as tribute.

BEN. Have you seen the play?

WILL. Which play?

BEN. A fusillade of fanciful fantasies called *What You Will.*

WILL. That was my subtitle for *Twelfth Night.*

BEN. He's indiscriminate, he steals from anyone.

WILL. Still, you have to grant him an innovative style.

BEN. Style? Those ugly grunts he substitutes for human speech? Those noxious neologisms he passes off as verse?

WILL. He is indeed unrivaled at torturing the English language.

BEN. If the Bishop of London had not banned literary satire, Marston would still be secreting his scurrilous poisons in penny bookstores, not on the public stage.

WILL. So the tables were turned, and you, the great mocker, were mocked.

BEN. As an oversexed scholar and morbid malcontent.

WILL. But Marston worships malcontents. Didn't he dedicate his play of that name to you?

BEN. He did say I was the model for his Malevole. But that foul wretch was stitched out of his own rotting soul, a pimple-assed coward who cannot even break wind without snarling.

(A chorus of breaking wind can be heard in **SHAKESPEARE**'s *cupboard.)*

Is that the villain in question stinking up your cupboard in there? Let's have him out. *(He goes off stage and returns, violently pulling the hapless* **MARSTON** *onto the floor, and snapping the whip around his cringing body.)*

MARSTON. Don't disfigure me, Ben. I beg of you.

BEN. I'll whip you into messes.

MARSTON. Beware! I bear a firearm fully cocked. Abuse me and I shall be obliged to discharge this lethal armament against your intimidating personage. *(Reaches into his pocket and pulls out a pistol. With his whip,* **JONSON** *snaps the pistol out of his hand, picks it up, and brandishes it.)*

BEN. You dare to pull a pistol on me!

MARSTON. Show clemency. I have a helpless spouse, two tender lambkins.

WILL. Be friends, you English fools. There are villains enough abroad, more deserving of your wrath.

BEN. *(putting the pistol in his belt)* I didn't come here to snuff him. I came here to purge him. The man stinks both inside and out. Will, fetch me that wash basin there.

(He drags **MARSTON** *to a chair, wraps a napkin around his neck, as if preparing him for barbering, thrusts a wash basin in his hands, throws a vial of liquid down his throat, holds his jaws shut and rubs his back until he swallows it, and stands behind him, choosing words from* **MARSTON**'s *writings,* **MARSTON** *whimpering throughout.)*

BEN. All right now, you paltry poltroon, prepare to disgorge all those ugly coinages you have lately been spewing into the public ear: "Oblitrant…furibund…turgidious."

MARSTON. *(choking)* "Oblitrant…furibund…turgidious."

BEN. "Glibbery…lubrical…defunct." Vomit them up!

MARSTON. "Glibbery…lubrical..defunct." Oh, I feel sick.

WILL. Be careful, Ben. Those polysyllabic hairballs could splinter his vocal chords.

BEN. *(unheeding)* Now these: "spurious…snotteries…chilblained."

MARSTON. "Spurious…snotteries…chilblained." Objection! "Chilblained" is a familiar medical utterance, linguistically legitimized…

BEN. Repeat! "Chilblained…obstupefact…fatuate."

MARSTON. "Chilblained…obstupefact…fatuate."

WILL. Have pity, Ben. I think all his gallstones have been spewed out by now.

BEN. *(to MARSTON)* Gagging, are we? Help yourself a little with your finger.

MARSTON. *(his finger down his throat)* Oh, oh, oh *(as if vomiting)* "prorumped…snarling guts…quaking custard."

BEN. Good.

WILL. *(pitying MARSTON)* Ben.

BEN. Enough for now. Your constitution partially restored, you are released forthwith, provided you keep your vocabulary free of loathsome Latinate locutions. For a restorative, I recommend daily readings in early English authors like Langland and Chaucer where you will learn to fuck, not fornicate, piss, not urinate, belch, not eructate, and fart, not flatulate–the last, God willing, out of smell-shot of civilized people. By night, you will study Horace regarding the true purpose of literature, which is to amuse and instruct, not abuse and insult. Should you need another purgative, eat your own plays.

MARSTON. *(getting out of the chair and throwing down the napkin and the basin)* I'll be revenged on you, Ben Jonson, I'll be revenged on the whole pack of you.

*(**MARSTON** storms out of the room and down the stairs.)*

WILL. He even stole his exit line–from my Malvolio.

BEN. Larcenous lout. A poet pissing against the wind.

WILL. Ben, you must learn to master your temper. You might have killed the beggar.

BEN. If I wanted to kill him, I would have peppered him with his own pistol. But it wasn't worth another prison term.

WILL. When did you serve in Newgate? Five years ago?

BEN. Seven next Shrovetide.

WILL. And all for engaging in a pointless duel. Why would you kill a poor actor?

BEN. Why, for being a poor actor.

WILL. Ben, you are sometimes subject to the most violent humours.

BEN. Not all of us can be meek and modest like our gentle Shakespeare here. You give offense to no one–least of all authority.

WILL. Offending people is not my purpose. I am no satirist.

BEN. That month in Newgate was a torment. Vermin in the bed. Worms in the food. Buggery in the jakes.

WILL. *(trying to ignore this)* A month was a very short sentence for a charge of manslaughter.

BEN. I pleaded benefit of clergy.

WILL. You a clergyman?

BEN. I managed to cough up enough Biblical Latin to confound the constabulary with my clerical skills. I was freed from all charges in return for an etching on my thumb. This one. *(showing his right thumb)*

WILL. M?

BEN. M for murderer. That's how our sainted sovereign rewarded her chosen playwright.

WILL. Nonsense, Ben, our late Queen Bess did ever hold you in the highest favor.

BEN. So long as I praised her royal maidenhead. I should have stayed an actor, like you, Will. By now, I would have earned a fellowship in a cry of players.

WILL. Perhaps our new king will increase the royal allowance to the playhouses.

BEN. Not for my kind of work. Our jejune Jamie, like your pompous Polonius, prefers a tale of bawdry or he sleeps.

WILL. *(hesitantly)* Last week, I received a summons from Whitehall. I suspect the King may want a play of me.

BEN. *(agitated with envy)* No, really? On what subject?

WILL. I have yet to be told.

BEN. More likely your invitation came from the Scottish King's Danish consort. Queen Anne is the real theatre enthusiast, and is paying a royal ransom for court masques. I have already dashed off two dozen for her, my major source of income.

WILL. Masques? I cannot abide those shallow spectacles.

BEN. Nor can I. But God gave us mouths to feed and stomachs to fill. And Queen Anne has inexhaustible fodder. The jewels she wore in *The Coronation Triumph* alone cost the treasury a hundred thousand pounds.

WILL. Write plays, man, not silly spectacles about dated Roman deities.

BEN. This from the man who cannot start a tragedy without the help of some ghostly apparition? *(acting the part with exaggeration)* "I am thy father's spirit, doomed for a certain time to walk the earth…"

WILL. *(impatiently interrupting)* Ghosts are legitimate theatrical devices, Ben, with roots in traditional Christian theology. But classical mythology is pure contrivance.

BEN. Had you acquired more learning, Will, you would speak less rubbish. But you're right about masques.

Machinery, treadmills, waterfalls, fireworks – no one listens to a play any more, they just ogle the costumes and go home singing the scenery.

WILL. Empty spectacle.

BEN. I envy your capacity for choice. My treasury is empty.

WILL. You've wasted your entire legacy?

BEN. Why else write masques? The remains of my meager savings were spent on burying my only son.

WILL. *(puts his arms around* **BEN** *to comfort him)* I buried a son, too, Ben. The worst thing that can happen to a man. But is your wife unable to bear another son?

BEN. My wife is a fallow plant. And yours?

WILL. Nearing fifty. Also past child-bearing.

BEN. Eight years your senior. Did you always fancy older women?

WILL. At eighteen, you fancy any woman who wiggles her body parts at you. And if you have the bad luck to impregnate one, you're bound to her for life. Twenty-three years of bondage in exchange for a few minutes of pleasure.

BEN. So that's why you left for London–to marry the theatre instead, and generate newborns twice every year upon the stage. No interest then in a return to Stratford?

WILL. No. No desire to settle into a glover's trade and spend my life raising children, like my Dad.

BEN. My story is the same. My stepfather was a bricklayer. But I had this hunger for learning and this talent for classical farce. What was I to do? Bake bricks instead of plays? Spend my life feeding ovens and furnaces?

WILL. *(raising his glass)* To the playhouse!

BEN. *(following suit)* To the playhouse!

WILL. To large visions…

BEN. …and small beer.

> *(A great deal of coughing and harumphing are heard off stage, and a loud voice shouting "Where is this lad? Where is this heart?")*

(An aging nobleman enters the room, the great Elizabethan courtier, **SIR JOHN HARINGTON**. *He goes directly to* **WILL** *and holds him by the shoulders, looking fondly into his eyes.)*

SIR JOHN. My dear Will. I expected to find you home.

WILL. And I would have thought you in Whitehall, dear Sir John.

SIR JOHN. No, sweet Will, I no longer much visit the court, unless commanded there by the Scot whose rump now fills the royal throne. No past favorite of the former Queen finds any favor with the present King.

WILL. *(to* **BEN***)* Ben, do you know this good old knight, the celebrated godson of our late Queen Bess? Sir John Harington, meet Ben Jonson.

BEN. A pleasure, Sir John. Your name and fame are legendary.

SIR JOHN. And so indeed are yours. I was on my feet in the theatre applauding your *Every Man In His Humour*.

BEN. And I was on my arse in the privy admiring your *Metamorphosis of Ajax*.

SIR JOHN. A perfect platform from which to view my modest labors.

WILL. Why's that?

BEN. Don't you know? This is the genius who invented the flushing toilet.

SIR JOHN. One of my cunningest contraptions.

WILL. Ajax. A jakes. How did I miss the pun in that title? From the depths of my bowels, I thank you.

BEN. Speaking of bowels, I must attend to mine. I was so busy purging Marston I neglected my own ablutions. And I still have a half-hour masque to write for our Queen Anne.

SIR JOHN. Farewell, Ben Jonson.

BEN. Goodbye, Sir John. And goodbye, Will. If you're ever in need of cash, think again about writing a masque for the Queen. *(embraces him and leaves)*

SIR JOHN. A great talent, but born for trouble.

WILL. I am unduly fond of the man.

SIR JOHN. And he of you, quite obviously. Indeed, the respect with which you are universally held is the reason I am here. What are your relations with the new crowd at court?

WILL. As yet untested, thus untroubled. King James has adopted our company, the Lord Chamberlain's Men, renaming it the Kings Men in return for a promise of royal patronage. On Tuesday, as it happens, I have been summoned to the palace to discuss a special project with him.

SIR JOHN. *(skeptical)* He is acquainted with your writing?

WILL. A play or two of mine has apparently kept him conscious for a while.

SIR JOHN. His approbation is predicated on one's good opinion of *him*. I visited court just a few days ago, summoned there on a scholar's errand. Contrary to all educated opinion, our King still holds a belief in witches. He has even written a treatise called *Daemonologie* approving the garroting of these innocent grannies. My approval of his brainless monograph was duly solicited. He was particularly concerned to know why witchcraft worked more powerfully on ancient women than on the young.

WILL. And your reply?

SIR JOHN. That according to Scripture, the devil likes to walk in dry places.

WILL. A merry answer.

SIR JOHN. He did not laugh.

WILL. No?

SIR JOHN. He is more given to Celtic barks than English guffaws. Aye me, what a transformation from the days of good Queen Bess.

WILL. In what way?

SIR JOHN. The Queen talked always of love and affection, this King preaches fear and submission. And his innovations! Did you know that court ladies now act upon the stage? Our good Queen Anne provides the example.

WILL. Women players! That *is* a novelty.

SIR JOHN. Our good King James is more aroused by male players. This ruler is much attracted to good looks and handsome accoutrements.

WILL. Who is his current favorite?

SIR JOHN. Robert Carr, who has publicly announced that the King's roan jennet surpasses Bucephalus and is worthy to be ridden by Alexander.

WILL. Flattery is nothing new at court.

SIR JOHN. What is new is a kingdom corrupt in its business dealings, dissolute in its sexual habits, intolerant in its religious practices- – the very conditions that you, Will Shakespeare, have been accustomed to condemn in your plays. And this brings me to my reason for coming. You want a commission? Write a play denouncing this dishonorable regime.

WILL. Denunciation is not my talent or my calling.

SIR JOHN. Then how explain your *Tragedy of Lear*, but three months past?

WILL. *(nervous)* That play was set in ancient times. It has nothing to do with our current regime.

SIR JOHN. *(pulls out a quarto of* King Lear *and reads)* "See how yond justice rails upon yond simple thief. Hark, in thine ear: change places, and, handy-dandy, which is the justice, which is the thief." Whose legal system are you describing there?

WILL. It is a comment on the legal system of ancient Britain.

SIR JOHN. I see. And this passage on the potent power of privilege? "Plate sin with gold/And the strong arm of justice hurtless breaks;/Arm it in rags, a pygmy's straw doth pierce it." Ancient Britain?

WILL. *(afraid)* Do you really believe that crazed old man on the heath was raging at the court of James?

SIR JOHN. Wasn't he? He should have been.

WILL. I do not hold it the proper function of a playwright to call for the overthrow of regimes, no matter how oppressive.

SIR JOHN. Then what is the proper function of the playwright, pray?

WILL. To reconfigure the way we look at the world, to enlighten the ignorant, to extend the imagination.

SIR JOHN. And your chief artistic obligation is–?

WILL. To hold a mirror up to nature.

SIR JOHN. Which makes your writing indistinguishable from milady's looking glass.

WILL. I am a dramatist, Sir John, and dramatists do not take sides. Their characters do. I simply record the discord in blank verse.

SIR JOHN. That is not enough, Will. Our world is in crisis. If playwrights do not quickly join in reforming an evil system, then they, along with all of England, will soon be buried by it.

WILL. I wish to go quietly about what is left of my life as a peaceful man of the theatre.

SIR JOHN. You cannot live in peace when others live in terror. I have not yet defined my own relationship to the persecuted Catholic recusants. But I know I cannot watch a Christian hang in chains while flatterers crawl up the ladder of preferment.

WILL. It was ever so.

SIR JOHN. It was never so like this. If you love your country, then you must begin to tell the truth about it. Otherwise, the squibs that fizzle harmlessly on your stage will start to explode in earnest on the street.

WILL. What are you suggesting? An armed rebellion? By whom?

SIR JOHN. The Catholic recusants.

WILL. I thought King Jamie had shown tolerance towards Rome.

SIR JOHN. Well, I cannot speak for his Danish Queen, who is rumored to have Papist sympathies. But James, brought up by Presbyterians, calls the Pope the Antichrist, and, like the Puritans, inveighs against the power of witches without believing in saints or miracles.

WILL. I have heard the King described as a devout man.

SIR JOHN. Oh, yes, he is devout–regarding his own godhead. His Majesty's favorite principle is the Divine Right of Kings, which in his case is rather like consecrating a baboon.

WILL. Sir John, forgive me, but we are not going to resolve the future of monarchy or the fate of religion through our debates.

SIR JOHN. I fear this debate will be resolved by hotter heads than ours. Since I obviously cannot move you, I will leave you. Meanwhile, I hope you can live comfortably with your conscience.

WILL. My conscience and I are perfectly compatible these days. And please do not confuse me with my characters. I am a simple law-abiding citizen trying to practice my art in an unsteady world.

SIR JOHN. Well, then, I will persecute you no longer, Will. But do not underestimate the power of your pen.

*(**SIR JOHN** leaves. **WILL** picks up his quill, looks at it, then throws it down angrily.)*

(lights down)

*(Lights up on a space in the Whitehall palace. **KING JAMES** and **QUEEN ANNE** sit on adjacent thrones like chess pieces, looking forward as they speak. They might as well be in separate countries. **JAMES** is drinking. Anne is reading a book, perhaps a Quarto of* As You LIke It. *After a moment, he looks up.)*

JAMES. Spouse.

ANNE. Your Britannic Divinity.

JAMES. Is it true what they tell me about young Prince Henry?

ANNE. Are we speaking again?

JAMES. Should you lie about this, we will *never* speak again.

ANNE. And your question?

JAMES. Whether the rumor is true that you locked up our twelve-year old son in the bedroom of one of your fleshier waiting women, who initiated him into the Court of Cupid.

ANNE. Who told you this?

JAMES. Why, every courtier knows it. It is the common chatter of the corridor.

ANNE. And does the corridor also chatter about the reason?

JAMES. For what possible reason would a mother, like a common bawd, introduce her male child to the temptations of the flesh?

ANNE. Is this exchange designed to end our estrangement?

JAMES. That estrangement was caused by you.

ANNE. No, by you, when you stole a baby from his mother's arms.

JAMES. You were a frivolous fourteen-year-old when we married, hardly suited to motherhood. You are thirty now, and still unready for that blessed state.

ANNE. You ripped my Henry from my breast at birth.

JAMES. And you reclaimed him through an act of criminal blackmail.

ANNE. Any mother prevented from seeing her own child would resort to desperate measures.

JAMES. Henry is the heir to my throne. He was not meant to be a plaything for a pampered princess.

ANNE. I am his mother.

JAMES. He was returned later to your arms.

ANNE. Five years later, and only after I threatened to return to Denmark.

JAMES. Typifying your willful, forward female nature.

ANNE. I gave you seven children –

JAMES. Four of whom did not survive their infancy. Not to mention your many miscarriages.

ANNE. *(exercised)* And who was to blame for that? My womb or this plague-infested land?

JAMES. You know why we never talk? Because you prefer to shout.

ANNE. I loved you once, James, young as I was. And believe you once loved me.

JAMES. Perhaps I did. That was a very long time ago.

ANNE. So now your affections wander like the moon.

JAMES. What does that mean?

ANNE. Your minions!

JAMES. *(defensive)* I know not what you mean.

ANNE. You have not visited my bedchamber a single night for many years, but your own bed is rarely empty. I could forgive your carnal knowledge of Anne Murray….

JAMES. This is dangerous talk.

ANNE. …but not your passion for Robert Carr.

JAMES. I feel only friendship for Robert Carr.

ANNE. You express this friendship through a bunghole.

JAMES. What are you saying, accursed woman? That your King is a Sodomite? Sodomy is expressly condemned in Leviticus 18:22.

ANNE. What does Leviticus 18:22 have to say about the secret passage between your bedroom and his?

JAMES. Carr is my trusted advisor. I require continual access to his counsel.

ANNE. At three o'clock in the morning? In your unbuttoned nightgown? The whole court knows how your favorite rules your heart. If I introduced young Henry to the pleasures of womankind, it was in hope he would not inherit his father's interest in the nether parts of men.

JAMES. Are you questioning the Divine Right of Kings?

ANNE. You invoke Divine Right, but the only divinity you truly worship is your own appetite.

JAMES. I have the power to divorce you, you know.

ANNE. Divorce me then. I am still dreaming of a return to Kronborg.

JAMES. I am a Stuart, not a Tudor. I have no intention of emulating the late Queen's much married father.

ANNE. And I have nothing to say in the matter?

JAMES. *(rising)* Nothing whatsoever. Such are my privileges under the Divine Right of Kings. Now pardon me, my Queen. I have more important state matters at hand than wrangling with a shrew.

(He exits. Anne begins to weep. After a few moments, **ROBERT CATESBY**, *a Catholic nobleman, thirty-two years old, handsome and bearded, steps from the shadows. He and* **ANNE** *embrace passionately.)*

CATESBY. The royal swine.

ANNE. You heard the king?

CATESBY. The king is no king, rather a lingering disease that calls for remedy.

ANNE. What do you mean?

CATESBY. To cure a diseased limb, they say, it must be chopped off.

ANNE. What is in your mind to provoke such violent imagery?

CATESBY. Question me no more, my dear one, till the deed be done.

ANNE. Tell me or not, I am already implicated.

CATESBY. Let me answer simply thus: I have a plan that would rid this land of despotism, and release us both from pain and torment. England would once again be free to practice its true faith.

ANNE. Are you planning my husband's death?

> (**CATESBY** *is silent.*)

ANNE. Be advised, I hate this tyrant morning, noon, and night. But I would not have him murdered.

CATESBY. I was thinking more of banishment.

ANNE. To where?

CATESBY. To where you would never see his face again.

ANNE. I have not truly seen his face in sixteen married years.

CATESBY. Then you are agreed?

ANNE. Providing my children be not harmed.

CATESBY. They will be safe from harm.

ANNE. Catesby, you will enjoy neither my love nor my protection, should the slightest danger touch upon my children.

CATESBY. *(taking her in his arms)* You are never to worry. Your children will be safe.

ANNE. *(more urgently)* And Prince Henry will be King. He will not be harmed.

CATESBY. That is our agreement.

ANNE. More than a profession of consent, I want your word of honor.

CATESBY. Insofar as anything is certain, Prince Henry will be King; Elizabeth and your younger son, Charles, will live. You have my sworn word.

> (*At this point,* **WILL** *walks into the room, surprised to find it occupied by* **ANNE** *and* **CATESBY**.)

CATESBY. And who are you, sirrah?

WILL. William Shakespeare. I beg forgiveness for interrupting your conference. I was told to meet the King in here.

ANNE. Shakespeare, the playwright?

WILL. Himself, your Majesty.

ANNE. I have seen your plays and much admired them.

WILL. I am deeply grateful, your gracious Majesty.

ANNE. Do you know him, Robert? The author of *As You Like It?*

CATESBY. I do not frequent playhouses.

ANNE. You have deprived yourself of much diversion.

WILL. I fear I have interrupted a private conference.

ANNE. No, it is we who are intruding. The King no doubt expects you here. Come, Catebsy. We will finish our business in the antechamber. *(to* WILL*)* Perhaps we can meet one other day and talk about your plays.

(SHAKESPEARE *bows. They exit.* WILL *looks round the room until* KING JAMES *enters with his customary bottle and glass.* WILL *kneels.)*

WILL. Your majesty.

JAMES. Get off the floor, Shakespeare. God knows when last they washed it.

WILL. Yes, my liege.

JAMES. Who was that departed with my Queen?

WILL. I know him not, your Majesty.

JAMES. It was Catesby, I warrant, a cat with needle claws. Well, my dear Shakespeare, how are you?

WILL. Very well, your Majesty, and deeply honored by this invitation.

JAMES. A dram of usquebagh? *(He offers* WILL *a drink.)*

WILL. Why thanks, your Majesty. *(He accepts the glass.)*

JAMES. One of the last remaining legacies of Scotland. *(downing one himself)* I am not a dedicated playgoer, but I have been much taken with your historical chronicles. You seem to have a scholar's appreciation for England's storied past.

WILL. I must confess I occasionally borrow histories from Holinshed.

JAMES. An excellent chronicler. But it is you who give his characters life.

WILL. You flatter me, your Majesty.

JAMES. I do not flatter my subjects.

WILL. No, of course not. Forgive my blunder.

JAMES. But I can reward them. How much do you know of Scottish history?

WILL. I know a bit about the exploits of the Bruce and of the Douglas.

JAMES. No, I mean the history of the Stuart succession.

WILL. Not much, I blush to say, your Majesty.

JAMES. The Scottish warriors, Banquo and his young son Fleance, started a whole line of kings. They are said to have been my ancestors.

WILL. I shall look them up in Holinshed.

JAMES. I want you to do more than look them up. I want you to write a play about them.

WILL. I see.

JAMES. There are some in this kingdom who still question my right to the throne. Your play might settle those doubts. You validated the royal rights of the Tudors for Elizabeth. I want you to do the same for me and the Stuarts.

WILL. *(hesitating)* An extraordinary honor, sir, I...

JAMES. Not an honor, your duty as a loyal servant of the crown.

WILL. I have always considered myself a...

JAMES. You're not a Papist, are you?

WILL. *(reddening)* Why, no, your Majesty. My father was the...

JAMES. Good. And what is your position on satanic witchcraft?

WILL. *(as if coached)* I abhor the practice and all things pertaining to the devil.

JAMES. Are you familiar with my book, *Demonologie?*

WILL. I have heard remarkable things about it, your Majesty, and have every intention of...

JAMES. Read it! Here is a copy, graced with the autograph of a king.

WILL. How can a poor subject ever thank a mighty monarch for such a signal honor?

JAMES. By writing witches into your play. There is too much doubt of their existence among the English, and you must help me teach them otherwise.

WILL. *(doubtfully)* Witches!

JAMES. I could hire your colleague Middleton to be your collaborator. *(WILL is silent.)* Thomas Middleton–the author of *The Witch*.

WILL. I know the man and am of course familiar with his play. I am confident I could handle the more fantastical aspects of the story myself.

JAMES. Fantastical, you say? Do you share the common doubts about these women, too?

WILL. *(hastily)* No, no, they are a bane upon the commonwealth.

JAMES. *(angrily, banging the table)* More than a bane, a sore, a blister, a carbuncle. Ever since Agnes Thompson roused storms to prevent the passage of my Queen from Denmark, I have been the subject of foul conspiracies. Did you know aught of this hag?

WILL. No, sir.

JAMES. She stole a linen cloth of mine, then bound a cat and christened it, tying it to dead parts of men, and threw it into the ocean to raise a tempest. Only my faith saved that ship from evil.

WILL. She confessed this?

JAMES. Of course she confessed it–after being duly persuaded. As additional proof of her evil nature, I, personally, discovered the devil's mark upon her private parts. The statute I passed last year makes it a capital offense to practice witchcraft in this realm, or even to exhume bodies for the sake of sorcery, charm, or enchantment. It's all in the book!

WILL. Yes, sir. And your loyal subjects are deeply grateful for the protection you provide them from these, uh, horrendous harridans.

JAMES. I would hope so. I would hope so. All right. Begin work on your play. And make it short! I abhor long nights at the theatre.

WILL. All sensible men do, your Majesty. I promise you my briefest work.

JAMES. The first performance of which will take place in the palace at Hampton Court. With all my English courtiers in obligatory attendance. How long till such a project reach the stage?

WILL. The actual writing would occupy me for, oh, perhaps half a year. The rehearsal period should be briefer. I believe the Kings Men could have the play prepared for you by next August.

JAMES. Sooner. I am an impatient man. Farewell, Shakespeare. And stop by the Secretary's office on your way out. He has a bag of gold coins there that should speed your enterprise.

WILL. No words can speak my gratitude.

JAMES. Then save them for your play.

(**SHAKESPEARE** *walks out of the King's chambers into his own. He is met there by* **SIR JOHN HARINGTON**, *who seems very upset.*)

WILL. The man's a menace. We are being ruled by a king whose governing handbook is a manual of sorcery.

SIR JOHN. That's why he's called the wisest fool in Christendom.

WILL. And he wants these witches to control the course of the action, even alter the design of history. Were I to assign such power to otherworldly creatures, every enlightened man in England would laugh me from the room.

SIR JOHN. Starting with me.

WILL. An object of ridicule!

SIR JOHN. You said No to him, of course.

WILL. Say No to a King?

SIR JOHN. You said No to me.

WILL. You are not a King.

SIR JOHN. Regardless, you must reject this assignment.

WILL. I might find a way to fold these creatures into the plot…

SIR JOHN. I seem to remember the purpose of drama was to hold a mirror up to nature.

WILL. These are different circumstances.

SIR JOHN. Because your looking glass is now reflecting the promise of preferment.

WILL. If I refuse the King's request, I could spend my middle age in the Tower, mourning my lost freedom, whereas if I shoveled in some scenes about a few fantastical women I could live out my life in peace and plenty. Writing about witches is hardly a mortal sin.

SIR JOHN. Are you forgetting all those wretched creatures even now being stretched upon the rack or hanging from the gibbet, while the great William Shakespeare labors to turn the King's delusions into deathless verse.

WILL. Sir John, I am by profession a poet and a playwright. My primary ambition is to fashion a good poem – and if possible avoid the rack myself.

SIR JOHN. You are a Kings man now, Will, in every sense of that phrase.

(enter **BEN JONSON**, *followed close upon by* **MARSTON***)*

BEN. Hallo, Will.

WILL. Now, now, Ben, no more purgations in this room.

BEN. No, Will, rest easy. Marston here and I are now the best of friends. Aren't we, Jack?

MARSTON. The most bountiful of brethren, the most compatible of companions.

WILL. What astronomical aberration accounts for this sudden change in feeling?

BEN. What else? A commission. Blackfriars has approached the two of us…

MARSTON. Actually, there's three of us.

BEN. …to write a city comedy for the Children of St. Paul's. Yes, there are three of us. We are collaborating with George Chapman. What a relief to be able to celebrate military courage and manly plain-dealing instead of courtly bowing and scraping.

MARSTON. *(looking admiringly on* **BEN***)* Once again, I am apprenticing the master.

BEN. And sharing his fat commission.

SIR JOHN. Well, that's happy news. Will, on the other hand, has just been commissioned by the King.

MARSTON. By the King!!

BEN. Has he told you yet the subject?

SIR JOHN. A vindication of the Stuart succession beginning with a procession of witches.

BEN. Why didn't he ask me? I know Scotland like the palm of my hand.

MARSTON. And I have comprehensive comprehension of witchcraft.

WILL. The King would like Tom Middleton to help me with the witches.

MARSTON. Let me manufacture the hellish harpies.

WILL. I am the man. And wish I weren't.

BEN. Come now, Will, don't be so punctilious. Royal patrimony is not so plentiful in these days of royal parsimony.

SIR JOHN. And it isn't every day one has the opportunity to flatter a degenerate king.

BEN. Degenerate is not the first word I would use to describe King Jamie. An idiot, yes, overly infatuated with his own meager learning, and easily hoodwinked. But basically your everyday royal dunce.

MARSTON. What's the plot of this play, Will?

BEN. Let him take an oath first not to steal it.

WILL. You know I have difficulty inventing plots. But I've found a few passages in Holinshed about a nobleman who kills his king and establishes an illegitimate claim to the throne.

MARSTON. His name?

WILL. Macbeth.

MARSTON. Sssssh.

WILL. What's the matter?

MARSTON. We don't pronounce those syllables anywhere near a theatre.

WILL. Why?

MARSTON. Nobody knows.

WILL. At all events, one of the nobleman this Mac–

MARSTON. Sssh.

WILL. This *Machiavel* slays is an ancestor of our own King James.

BEN. Name of –?

WILL. Banquo. Father of Fleance, founder of the Stuart line.

MARSTON. And whence come the witches?

WILL. *(picking up Holinshed and reading)* According to Holinshed, this thane Mac –

BEN & MARSTON. Ssssh.

WILL. This nameless Scottish thane and Banquo encounter three women in strange and wild apparel, "resembling creatures of the elder world, nymphs or fairies" who hail him future King of Scotland.

BEN. So in place of your customary ghastly ghosts, you'll now be featuring withered witches?

WILL. That's the challenge – having both. I am thinking of bringing the spirit of Banquo back from the dead to frighten the usurper.

BEN. *Hamlet, revenge!!*

MARSTON. Nymphs and fairies are not witches.

WILL. Holinshed refers to them as "weird sisters."

MARSTON. I have a weird sister but I wouldn't call her a witch. *(thinks)* Maybe I would.

BEN. Enough with nymphs and witches and Marston's weird relatives, I think our friend has a play here.

WILL. *(encouraged)* I found a later passage in Holinshed regarding another Scottish noble, name of Donwald, who also kills his king. With the help of a wife more murderous than he.

BEN. A regicidal Scot with a homicidal wife. Better and better.

SIR JOHN. Will, I believe you are collecting materials here for a marvelous monument to monomania – therefore one that will doubtless please the King.

WILL. I believe I am developing something more, Sir John, that may please the King without disgracing me.

SIR JOHN. The King is the disgrace, and you will be, too, if you stage this travesty. How do you propose to satisfy at the same time the demands of your patron and the principles of your art?

WILL. Ah. And that, Sir John, remains a mystery, like the prohibition on my hero's name.

BEN & MARSTON. Sssh.

(**SIR JOHN** *shakes hands and leaves. The others remain in darkness. On the street,* **SIR JOHN** *is met by* **ROBERT CATESBY.**)

CATESBY. Well-met, Sir John.

SIR JOHN. I hope we are well-met, Catesby. You asked for this meeting, not I. How goes your cause?

CATESBY. It proceeds apace. Any decision yet about joining our movement against this Scottish heretic?

SIR JOHN. You know how strongly I believe in every Christian's right to worship.

CATESBY. I am not interested in toleration. I am interested in change.

SIR JOHN. But any change you consider must be based on the principle of religious freedom.

CATESBY. What chance is there for religious freedom in a time of Protestant constraint?

SIR JOHN. Very little, I fear. The last Hampton Court Conference represented a total capitulation to the Puritans.

CATESBY. As a final insult, I am told, James is planning to translate the Holy Bible into colloquial English and name the heretical text after himself.

SIR JOHN. A King James version of the Latin Vulgate. More of his monstrous egotism.

CATESBY. Better say, apostasy.

SIR JOHN. That kind of apostasy, Catesby, is a lot less dangerous than the imprisonment of priests, the torture of old women, and the oppression of recusants.

CATESBY. We are planning an action that would conclusively and forever protect our Catholic brethren from official persecution.

SIR JOHN. Nay, if it involves sedition, tell me no more. As a peer of the realm, I am obliged to report all treasonous acts to the crown.

CATESBY. How else would you suggest we rid the land of this intolerable tyrant? By paying his passage back to Edinburgh on a packet boat?

SIR JOHN. That question is for you to answer. In regard to any rebellion or mutiny, I must turn a deaf ear.

CATESBY. I trust your hearing is sufficiently impaired to block out everything thus far spoken.

SIR JOHN. I have heard nothing. Therefore, I can reveal nothing.

CATESBY. *(sarcastically)* The perfect conditions for political apathy – deafness and dumbness. You are a man who would condemn injustice, while doing nothing to end it. There is a political label for such impotent reformers. *Trimmers!*

SIR JOHN. *(stung)* Sir John Harington has always been in the vanguard of resistance to oppressive government. But I believe in deliberate and effective change, not hopeless gestures by violent extremists.

CATESBY. Which means you want others to launder your dirty linen, while you enjoy the purity of a spotless life.

SIR JOHN. You consider my motives to be impure? Then let me ask you this. Is your antipathy towards our inebriate King stimulated by his religious policies or by the fact that you are fucking his Queen?

(A long silence. Murderous stares.)

CATESBY. Farewell, Sir John. You have promised to hold your tongue about our meeting.

SIR JOHN. I pledge not to reveal the nature of your objective.

CATESBY. And I pledge not to reveal the objectionableness of your nature. Adieu. *(He leaves.)*

(SIR JOHN *remains reflectively looking into the audience.)*

(He joins **BEN** *and* **MARSTON** *in a tavern.)*

SIR JOHN. I fear that some monstrous act is being concocted against the state.

BEN. That is what we do. It is called playwriting.

MARSTON. What monstrous act?

SIR JOHN. One that could result in the loss of many lives.

BEN. Real lives? Now that is admittedly something else. Playwrights are more accustomed to butchering people with bladders of sheep's blood.

SIR JOHN. There is human blood enough being shed in the Old Palace Yard.

BEN. Which is why the spectators spend more time at the scaffold than at the theatre. The imagination of the playwright can invent nothing to equal the artistry of the executioner.

MARSTON. I am in complete compatibility with the groundlings on that issue. The gallows! What a spectacle! Heart on a dagger. Head on a pike. Bowels in a barrel. Unsurpassable.

BEN. You should have been a Roman, Marston.

MARSTON. Some say I am descended from Seneca the Younger, who severed his veins in the bathtub with a razor.

BEN. And some say you are descended from his bloody bathwater.

MARSTON. Still mocking me, Ben? Why? I loved you ever.

BEN. So what is this monstrous deed, Sir John?

SIR JOHN. I made a vow not to reveal it; yet, I wonder if it is not my duty to inform the King about the plots being hatched against his life.

BEN. What plots are those?

SIR JOHN. I have no idea.

BEN. Then how can you inform the King? You'll only end up in the Star Chamber being tortured for information you do not possess.

SIR JOHN. Thanks for that advice. After all, what do we owe this Scottish muttonhead.

BEN. Careful. Will is writing a play about this Scottish muttonhead.

SIR JOHN. A capitulation to the powers that be.

BEN. Why capitulation? It is a playwright's function to fashion plays.

SIR JOHN. Just as it is a opportunist's function to flatter kings.

(enter **WILL***)*

WILL. Well, as it happens, this opportunist has just completed a scene about three murderers hired by a king. *(calling)* Francis!

(A voice answers: "Anon, anon, sir.")

BEN. Three? You told me two.

WILL. The third murderer is an enigma to me, too. He just materialized into the action – like a specter.

BEN. You didn't write him?

WILL. My hand did, but not my brain. Sometimes I think this play is writing me.

MARSTON. *The Malcontent* wrote me.

BEN. From an inkwell filled with shit and bile. Explain yourself, Will. I never created a character I couldn't control.

WILL. Well, you know my skepticism regarding witches. But lately those weird sisters have been taking over my waking and dreaming life, issuing from my mind like creatures that look not like the inhabitants of the earth, and yet are on it.

SIR JOHN. King Jamie will be overjoyed to hear how you have endorsed his supernatural fantasies.

WILL. Don't scorn the supernatural, Sir John. It is the warehouse of dreams, the oven of the imagination. The other night I had a terrifying nightmare that froze the very hairs upon my head.

MARSTON. The substantiality?

WILL. An army of owls was attacking falcons, and horses were breaking their stalls, running wild and eating each other.

BEN. You dazzled the groundlings with phenomena like that in *Julius Caesar*. Put it in your new play.

WILL. It is in the play.

MARSTON. Oh, why did I not think of the inspired implausibility of flesh-eating horses!

WILL. They are murdering my sleep.

SIR JOHN. And this you call a "mere commission"?

WILL. A playwright cannot write according to another's dictation. Eventually, he must commit himself to the project and take charge of it. Or else admit that the project is taking charge of him. This one has me in a mighty grip. I am going back to work. *(downs his drink)*

(Lights dim as the other characters leave, and **WILL** *walks back to his desk and starts writing. After a few moments,* **QUEEN ANNE,** *disguised as a boy, knocks upon his door.* **WILL** *lets her in.)*

WILL. Yes?

ANNE. Do you require another boy actor for your plays. I have considerable experience and an unbroken voice.

WILL. We hold auditions in the Spring, at the South Bank.

ANNE. *(smiling)* Do you not recognize me? *(She takes off her cap and shakes her hair free.)*

WILL. *(down on one knee)* Your Majesty! I am speechless. Is it safe for you to appear thus unattended in Cripplegate?

ANNE. No more dangerous than navigating the corridors of court. Pretend I am Rosalind in doublet and hose visiting Orlando in the Forest of Arden.

WILL. Teaching him how to write poetry?

ANNE. I thought she was teaching him how to make love. But it is you who must instruct me in the subjects you have mastered.

WILL. Poetry or love?

ANNE. *(embarrassed)* I mean the motives that drive the human heart.

WILL. You are welcome to whatever advice my poor imagination can muster, Madame. But why came you here?

ANNE. We cannot meet in court. My husband has put spies on me. Hence this disguise.

WILL. Then tell me how I can help you.

ANNE. I need your insight into the destiny of kings.

WILL. You are writing a play?

ANNE. No, but you are, I am told. On the subject of my husband's succession to the throne.

WILL. Ah, you've heard about my *Tragedy of Macbeth?*

ANNE. So that is your murderer's name?

WILL. When I'm allowed to pronounce it.

ANNE. Tell me about this Scottish villain.

WILL. He gains the throne by killing the good king Duncan. And preserves it by wallowing in a sea of blood.

ANNE. Does he have a wife, this fatal pretender?

WILL. Yes, a woman with a powerful will, who reinforces his weaker intention with her superior resolve. I have just completed a speech in which she quickens his flagging intent.

ANNE. May I read it?

WILL. Yes, please. I need to hear it spoken.

ANNE. "I have given suck and know how tender 'tis/To love the babe that milks me:/I would, while it was smiling in my face,/Have plucked my nipple from his boneless gums,/And dashed the brains out, Had I so sworn as you/Have done to this."

WILL. The hairs are crawling on the back of my neck You speak those lines with such startling power.

ANNE. To speak them is one matter. To do them is another.

WILL. What mother could?

ANNE. Not I. *(pause)* But I do know how your lady feels.

WILL. You do?

ANNE. They once plucked my baby from my breast by order of the King.

WILL. His own child?

ANNE. Let me play the murderer's wife. I could act that part, with powerful conviction…

WILL. Madam, I do not doubt your talent…

ANNE. – a lot more convincingly than any squeaking boy.

WILL. …but, as you are aware, women are not permitted to appear upon the London stage.

ANNE. I have acted and danced in eighteen masques at Hampton Court.

WILL. And been much acclaimed for your theatrical skills. But there you performed within the protected confines of the court, not in a public playhouse under the watchful eye of the civil authorities.

ANNE. Explain the strange prohibition that prevents English women from acting on a public stage.

WILL. It is the prejudice of Puritans, for whom the public exposure of the female form is equivalent to a mortal sin.

ANNE. Puritans are not very fond of women.

WILL. Except when they are cooking or breeding.

ANNE. Nor are they tolerant towards plays.

WILL. True. They care for music, which they consider sacred, but if the Puritans were to gain power in England, God forbid, their first official act would be to shutter the public playhouses.

ANNE. And banish women from the public streets. Already those lustful hypocrites are admonishing us to cover our bosoms, shroud our faces, and conceal our hair under shawls.

WILL. Can you imagine making theatre under those conditions?

ANNE. Can you imagine making love under those conditions?

WILL. I can imagine making love to a beautiful woman under any conditions.

ANNE. *(pause)* Then you don't consider the female body a temptation to sin?

WILL. I consider it the most perfect thing in nature, especially in the shape that appears before me now.

ANNE. *(coming closer to him in a vaguely seductive way)* Is there nothing I can do to win a part in your new play?

WILL. I fear I cannot alter statutes, your Majesty. *(a thought)* Perhaps a private performance might be possible.

ANNE. *(flirtatious)* For you alone? And what would you have me wear?

WILL. *(embarrassed)* No, no, I mean a production of one of my plays at court, funded by the Crown. It would take place outside the jurisdiction of the city fathers and be no more costly than one of your masques.

ANNE. I am sorry you mentioned cost.

WILL. Forgive me, your Majesty.

ANNE. I know I am regarded as a frivolous and extravagant woman...

WILL. Not so, your Majesty.

ANNE. I know I am. But the large amounts I spend on theatrical presentations are not wasted. They humanize a court known otherwise for drunkenness and lechery.

WILL. Madame, I am certain that is so.

ANNE. Master Shakespeare, if you can not write a play for me, would you at least write for me a masque?

WILL. I feel honored to be asked, your Highness. But masques are not my forte.

ANNE. Ben Jonson has written two dozen at my request.

WILL. I'll tell you what, your Majesty. While I am not by temperament a masque-writer, I might include some masque-like elements in my future work.

ANNE. You would do that?

WILL. I am sketching a series of romances about the reconciliation of fathers and daughters, each reunion celebrated with a brief climactic spectacle. Why not a masque? After citing Jupiter and Juno, though, and a nod or two to Ceres, I am afraid my catalogue of Roman deities would be exhausted.

ANNE. Then ask Thomas Middleton to introduce you to Hecate.

WILL. As a matter of fact, your husband has already commissioned Middleton to plunk Hecate in the middle of my Scottish tragedy.

ANNE. An odd place to find a Roman Queen of the Underworld.

WILL. My sentiments exactly, Madame. But my play is also about present-day witches.

ANNE. Ah, that I should have guessed. My husband never misses an opportunity to exercise his obsessions.

WILL. Yes, but now the King's obsessions are becoming my own.

ANNE. Is that a reference to witchcraft? Or to me? *(***WILL** *is silent. They look intensely into each other's eyes.)*

(Lights up on **GUY FAWKES,** *also known as* **JOHN JOHNSON.** *He lets out a whistle. Silence. Another whistle. The whistle is returned from off stage. Enter* **CATESBY.***)*

FAWKES. *(very conspiratorial)* I was ordered to meet a man on the Bankside with a golden medal around his neck. Your medal looks more bronze than gold.

CATESBY. Time has tarnished it.

FAWKES. Like my features. What is your name?

CATESBY. My name is Catesby.

FAWKES. Christian name?

CATESBY. Robert.

FAWKES. I believe you are the man I am to meet.

CATESBY. And you, I believe, are the notorious Guy Fawkes.

FAWKES. *(very conspiratorial)* Hush. Hereabouts I am known as John Johnson. But I prefer the name of Guido.

CATESBY. Why?

FAWKES. *(very conspiratorial)* It is my code name.

CATESBY. Well, Guido, I am told you have some cunning as a mining engineer.

FAWKES. Aye, sir. A profession I prepared for in the military service.

CATESBY. You are a soldier?

FAWKES. A soldier no longer. I was cashiered.

CATESBY. Sir Thomas Percy tells me –

FAWKES. Hush. All participants remain anonymous.

CATESBY. My anonymous friend tells me you have a specialty –

FAWKES. Hush. Call it a mystery. I know how to release vast quantities of heat and pressure into the atmosphere, accompanied by loud noises.

CATESBY. I believe most of us have that capacity.

FAWKES. *(even more conspiratorial)* Aha, we do indeed. But how many of us can follow a discharge of intestinal gas with a blast of deadly petar?

CATESBY. And you have been acquainted with our purpose?

FAWKES. To blow up the Houses of Parliament and kill the King.

CATESBY. That is our ambition.

FAWKES. A volatile ambition. Why Parliament?

CATESBY. Parliament is the seat of all the mischief they have done to us; therefore, God has chosen that place for their punishment.

FAWKES. Amen to that. The explosive materials *(whispered)* are to be conveyed *(normal voice)* up the river Thames *(whispered)* and will arrive within the week by rowboat.

CATESBY. Is your accumulation of gunpowder sufficient for the task?

FAWKES. Let us not use that incriminating word "gunpowder." Let us rather call it "black residue."

CATESBY. Well, then, is your supply of black residue sufficient for the task?

FAWKES. More than sufficient. When all my barrels are successfully ignited, then everything in the old Palace, Westminster Abbey included, would be reduced to pebbles.

CATESBY. I am most concerned about the House of Lords.

FAWKES. Oh, yes, the House of Lords will be rubbled, but also, you should know, the House of Commons, too. A charge like that, judiciously placed, would cause both towers to buckle, break, and fall like ashes into the Thames.

CATESBY. If the Commons falls, I fear me a number of fellow religionists will also die in the blast.

FAWKES. In the course of such events, the innocent often suffer with the guilty. Have you sought clerical counsel on this matter?

CATESBY. I have made confession to Father Henry Garnet.

FAWKES. Sssh. No names. And the unidentified priest's response?

CATESBY. The same as yours. To my question whether it was lawful to involve the destruction of the innocent together with the guilty the anonymous father answered in the affirmative, giving as illustration the fate of townspeople besieged in time of war.

FAWKES. So you have his promise not to inform?

CATESBY. Yes, he is obliged by canonical law to maintain the secrets of the confessional. Indeed, he has published a tract about Equivocation which defends one's right to conceal any evidence of treason.

FAWKES. Under all circumstances?

CATESBY. Under all circumstances.

FAWKES. Even under torture?

CATESBY. If I know my anonymous father.

FAWKES. Then the secrets of our enterprise are safe.

CATESBY. Provided you are able to conceal your quantity of explosives until the appointed hour.

FAWKES. Our thirty-six barrels of gunpowder…

CATESBY. Black residue.

FAWKES. Corrected! We will hide our thirty-six barrels of black residue in the cellar of the Parliament building.

CATESBY. How do you expect to smuggle a packet that large into Westminster?

FAWKES. Well, our first thought was to drive a mine into the interior from an adjacent building. But then we met the coal maker who leases the Parliament cellar, and persuaded him to rent the space to us.

CATESBY. How did you persuade him?

FAWKES. With the sanction of our blesséd Redeemer, we cut his throat. The room now awaits our product.

CATESBY. And the odds against the King surviving?

FAWKES. Next to nil. Not a soul will remain alive. The King and his family will be blown back to the northern mountains, and the bishops and all the Protestant lords rattled down to hell like a shuttle of coal.

CATESBY. The Queen is not to be harmed.

FAWKES. Why spare the giddy consort of an evil despot?

CATESBY. She is of our movement.

FAWKES. How's that? Is the Queen a Catholic?

CATESBY. She was born a Lutheran, but now leans towards Rome. Although not yet baptized, she received a rosary from the Pope himself two years ago.

FAWKES. And that explains her sympathy for our cause?

CATESBY. That, and her distaste for the man she married.

FAWKES. Perhaps she has found a Catholic protector?

(**CATESBY** *glowers.*)

Clearly a delicate topic.

CATESBY. I find this line of inquiry rude and objectionable. Her children's safety is a condition of her consent.

FAWKES. You have mentioned that already. So who is to be our sanctioned Heir Apparent?

CATESBY. We intend to crown Princess Elizabeth the Catholic Queen of England.

FAWKES. A nine year old girl. Does that have the Queen's consent?

(**CATESBY** *is silent.*)

FAWKES. We might sequester the royal children before the blast occurs…

CATESBY. We will sequester Princess Elizabeth only. The absence of the two male royals from the opening of Parliament would excite too many questions. After all, Henry is Prince of Wales, next in line of the royal succession.

FAWKES. We could distract attention from his murder.

CATESBY. How?

FAWKES. By sparking a popular revolt in the Midlands.

CATESBY. Mr. Fawkes…

FAWKES. Johnson.

CATESBY. Guido. Your dedication is admirable, but our immediate intention is to blow up Parliament and kill the King. The civil war will follow in due course.

FAWKES. Blow up Parliament and kill the King. That should occupy our leisure hours at present. And your Queen consort can occupy your leisure hours thereafter.

(Lights up on:)

(WILL*'s quarters in Cripplegate. He is writing.)*

(A knock on the door. It is **QUEEN ANNE** *disguised again as a boy.)*

WILL. Your Majesty. I am heartily glad you came. I have just now been finishing my portrait of a truly harrowing Queen.

ANNE. Your Scottish Lady?

WILL. Indeed, descending into madness.

ANNE. Madness! How does that manifest itself?

WILL. Through visions of blood spots on her hands which cannot be removed.

ANNE. She sounds in severe distress.

WILL. She is.

ANNE. And so indeed am I.

WILL. Heaven forbid. May I be of help?

ANNE. No, it is an affliction of my own making.

WILL. Can I offer nothing?

ANNE. Only your sympathy. Talk to me of patience. Teach me how to survive an unbearable union without losing my mind.

WILL. Your marriage is such a trial?

ANNE. It is an agony. The King is callow, callous, cruel. We have not shared a bed these sixteen years, except to procreate children.

WILL. Royal marriages are almost never happy.

ANNE. I was barely fourteen, an instrument of policy, forced into the arms of a man I had never met in a land I had never seen.

WILL. Was there never any chance of love between you?

ANNE. For a moment once. When ferocious storms blocked my passage from Denmark, James came to rescue me with a retinue three hundred strong. He held me in his arms and kissed me–the only tender moment in all our years of wedlock.

WILL. The King told me of those storms. He blamed them on a witch.

ANNE. I have become the witch he blames.

WILL. There is no doubt you are bewitching.

ANNE. *(moving towards* **WILL***)* Have I bewitched you, Will Shakespeare?

WILL. *(Pause. He is very tempted.)* I am bound unto another Anne, your Majesty.

ANNE. From what I hear, that has hardly been an obstacle before.

WILL. I cannot defile her bed again.

ANNE. And what explains this sudden fever of fidelity?

WILL. *(pause)* There are other obstacles. Your Majesty.

ANNE. Yes?

WILL. The King, your husband.

ANNE. The King, my husband? Yes?

WILL. *(relieved)* Under other circumstances, your Majesty….

ANNE. *(shortly)* Of course. I await the time when English manhood may once again be fearless.

*(*WILL *ashamed, says nothing.)*

ANNE. Will, tell me, is your Anne ever in your heart?

WILL. Indeed, she has been too little in my thoughts.

(sounds upon the stairs)

SIR JOHN. *(off)* Will, are you there?

WILL. Forgive me, your Majesty, you must leave now. Quickly. *(loudly)* Yes, we'll work further on that wooing scene next week.

*(*WILL *opens the door for* ANNE. SIR JOHN HARINGTON *enters, with a letter in his hand.)*

WILL. Sir John, I give you welcome. I was just bidding farewell to one of our boy actors.

(shakes ANN*'s hand and she leaves)*

SIR JOHN. Will, I must have your counsel, this moment.

WILL. You are much aroused, Sir John.

SIR JOHN. I have been secretly informed that Robert Catesby had been planning to murder hundreds of nobles, myself included, by means of a violent attack on the houses of Parliament.

WILL. How learned you this?

SIR JOHN. From my brother-in-law, Francis Tresham. *(reads from the letter)* "I advise you to devise some excuse not to attend this Parliament, for they shall receive a terrible blow, and yet shall never see who hurts them."

WILL. How did Tresham learn of this conspiracy?

SIR JOHN. I fear he is part of it.

WILL. And out of concern for your safety, he advises you to wait out the event at home?

SIR JOHN. Yes, advice for which I owe him my life.

WILL. You must expose this attack.

SIR JOHN. I have already done so. Instantly. The moment I received the letter I alerted the watch to search

Parliament. In the cellar they found a tremendous cache of gunpowder being superintended by a knave named John Johnson. He had a timepiece, slow matches, and touch paper in his possession.

WILL. (*to himself*) My third murderer.

SIR JOHN. This is no play, Will.

WILL. How close was he to setting off the gunpowder, this Johnson knave?

SIR JOHN. Minutes away. And far from denying his intentions, he boasted of his plan to murder the King and destroy all government buildings, meanwhile advising the arresting officers to speak in lowered tones.

WILL. A curious villain.

SIR JOHN. My question now is what to do with Tresham's incriminating letter, which he urges me to burn.

WILL. You must not burn it. You must show the letter to the King. You have saved his life and that of countless innocents. Now you must expose the wretches responsible for this plot.

SIR JOHN. That is the counsel I was hoping for, Will, though it makes me complicit in the arrest of my close relative and Robert Catesby and God knows how many other friends. I hardly consider myself either loyal to the government or faithful to the Crown. But I do believe myself a patriotic Englishman, and that means rooting out the culprits, no matter how close in friendship or in blood. The regime must be changed.

WILL. How?

SIR JOHN. I don't know how. But not through violence.

(*lights down*)

(*When the lights come up we see* **ANNE** *and* **KING JAMES** *sitting on their thrones.* **JAMES** *wears the wig and robes of a high court judge, while carrying his usual bottle of whiskey.* **GUY FAWKES** *stands before the king–in chains.*)

JAMES. So you are the villain John Johnson.

ANNE. *(ANNE makes as if to go.)* Do you really need me here to witness this?

JAMES. Yes, yes, my dear, I expressly want your witness. So you are John Johnson?

FAWKES. No, your Holy Magistrate, I am Guy Fawkes.

JAMES. Well, then, you villain of multiple names, I intend to put some questions to you. And I command you to be open about this conspiracy.

FAWKES. A conspiracy is secret by its very nature.

JAMES. I am your King.

FAWKES. And thus you can command the truth?

JAMES. And thus I can command your death. Was it your intention and that of your confederates, in a fearsome act of terror, to blow up the House of Lords?

FAWKES. The truth?

JAMES. Yes.

FAWKES. Both the House of Lords and the House of Commons. And every Protestant heathen inside their walls.

JAMES. Myself included, I assume.

FAWKES. Including your heretical self, and all your periwigged Lords.

JAMES. *(smacks him across the face)* There is no need for seditious insults.

ANNE. Prince Henry and Prince Charles, as well?

FAWKES. Your apostate bastard brats as well.

(JAMES *slaps him again.*)

ANNE. *(in a state of shock)* I must leave this place.

JAMES. No, I want you to witness what these heretics are capable of. Now Guy Fawkes or John Johnson or whatever is your name of choice at the moment....

FAWKES. I also answer to the name of Guido...

JAMES. ...I must demand...

FAWKES. ...but only to my confederates...

JAMES. …the names of your confederates.

FAWKES. You are at liberty to demand of me whatever you will, except compliance. I am not a flowing stream of information.

JAMES. No, you are a swollen sewer of sedition.

FAWKES. Say, rather, a liberal libation of liberation.

JAMES. *(ignoring the remark)* Is the name of Robert Winter familiar to you?

FAWKES. The name of Robert is familiar, and winter, if I do not mistake me, is the coldest of our seasons. Its solstice is coming on apace and will arrive in approximately six weeks. Brr.

JAMES. How about Sir Thomas Percy?

(**FAWKES** *is silent.*)

Lord John Grant? Sir Ambrose Rokewood?

(*silence from* **FAWKES**)

Do you know Robert Catesby?

(**ANNE** *visibly starts.*)

FAWKES. *(looking at* **ANNE***)* I know a cuckoo knows him.

JAMES. *(angry)* Have you also heard that he is dead.

(**ANNE** *is working hard to control herself.*)

JAMES. Shot in Staffordshire like a common criminal, following an attempted revolt in the Midlands.

FAWKES. The Midlands always was a revolting place.

JAMES. This coldhearted coward was forever skulking around the antechambers, lurking in corridors, preparing to bring disgrace upon the honor of England.

FAWKES. More than you could possibly know.

(**ANNE** *stares stolidly ahead.* **FAWKES** *remains silent.*)

JAMES. My agents tell me there were at least thirteen devil-worshipping conspirators involved in this wicked plot. I expect you to name me all their names.

FAWKES. I wish I could satisfy your passion for information but I am subject to serious memory lapses.

JAMES. Perhaps we can cure you of that affliction.

FAWKES. I assume we are now speaking of enhanced interrogation procedures?

JAMES. You may make no such assumption. Torture is prohibited in this kingdom.

FAWKES. Well, you have kept that prohibition a closely guarded secret.

JAMES. I say it is prohibited. Unless expressly commanded by the monarch or the Privy Council.

FAWKES. And my case of course would justify such expedients.

JAMES. Starting, of course, with the gentler applications, like the rack and the thumbscrew.

FAWKES. And following those merciful activities?

JAMES. *Et sic per gradus ad maiora tenditur.*

FAWKES. What the hell does that mean?

JAMES. It means, rude person, "And then by steps extend to more advanced interrogation procedures."

FAWKES. So the chief agent of justice in this kingdom is also the chief agent of torture. Your Royal Thumbscrew.

JAMES. *(getting angry)* You were preparing to obliterate an entire vested government, including some of the greatest statesmen in Europe. It is my duty to wring a confession from you by whatever means available.

FAWKES. It is a comfort that your religion expressly forbids inflicting pain on other human beings.

JAMES. And were you not planning to maim and murder hundreds of other human beings in the name of *your* religion? Is that why our Saviour died upon the cross? To satisfy the blood lust of a miscreant like you?

FAWKES. No more theology. Do your worst.

JAMES. I will. It was God himself prevented this unprecedented disaster to our kingdom. Many likeminded villains are still at large. We must root them out. I herewith declare a war on terror, and swear to arm our nation with every defense available. Let us start with the rack.

FAWKES. Bring it on. I look forward to the exercise. I have not stretched in years.

(lights down)

(Lights up on The Mermaid Tavern. WILL *is at a table, drinking with* SIR JOHN. *His spirits are very low, and he's a little drunk.)*

WILL. Oh, why did I ever waste my legacy in words instead of drink? Who gives tuppence for the stage these days, with the groundlings stampeding each other for a clearer view of the executions on Tower Hill.

SIR JOHN. Were you at the Fawkes hanging?

WILL. I have no taste for sanctioned murders.

SIR JOHN. That death you should have witnessed. He made a notable end. No torture could open his mouth. And at the moment the hangman fixed the noose around his neck, he leaped from the scaffold and executed himself.

WILL. Thus depriving the spectators of the satisfaction of watching his privates being cut off and burnt while the man was still alive. What is it in the human heart that finds such pleasure in another's pain?

SIR JOHN. A passion to see the privileged suffer.

WILL. Accompanied by religious sentiments of pity and forgiveness.

SIR JOHN. Not all religions, surely.

WILL. It is of no matter which faith you choose. All paths lead to the same charnel house.

SIR JOHN. That sounds very close to blasphemy.

WILL. Perhaps. *(wearily)* But my pickled brain is slowly coming to grasp… (WILL *goes into a drunken fugue state.)*

SIR JOHN. Well what, man?

WILL. *(coming to himself)* …coming to grasp…that faith partly exists to sanctify murder. The Catholics chant *Blessed be Our Redeemer, Death to the Unbeliever.* The Protestants scream *God Save the King, Death to the Papist.* The Mohammedans howl *God is Great, Death to the Infidel.* Yes, even the Gunpowder Plotters believed they would be welcomed into Paradise for blowing Protestant royals to bits. We have always been told that the only earthly evil is Machiavellian atheism. But evil circumscribes both the blessed and the damned.

SIR JOHN. You left out the Jews.

WILL. *Blessed art thou, oh God, King of the universe, Pour forth Thy wrath upon the nations that do not recognize Thee.* All the orthodoxies share the same vindictive mottoes.

SIR JOHN. You are either very dejected or very drunk.

(WILL *shrugs.*)

Perhaps you need another? *(calling)* Francis!

(WILL *gives another shrug as Francis calls, "Anon, anon, sir.")*

SIR JOHN. Look you, the sun shines still.

WILL. Yes, the sun shines still. But when the darkness falls, I gaze up at heaven and see only cold elusive stars.

SIR JOHN. You have caught a touch of Hamlet's melancholy. Shake it off, man. God and his angels inhabit the heavens, and humanity is basically good. It is the tyrannical rulers who turn men into beasts.

WILL. Or is it the beast in men's hearts that turns rulers into tyrants? If the heavens do not quickly tame these vile offenses, humanity must perforce prey upon itself, like monsters of the deep.

SIR JOHN. You should write that into your plays.

WILL. I already have. It is in the damp white hairs of King Lear. It is in the crooked spine of Richard the Third. It is in the twisted intellect of Ensign Iago. And now it has entered the infected blood stream of my Scottish hero who tells us human life is a tale told by an idiot, full of sound and fury, signifying nothing.

(They look at each other for a few moments in silence. During these last speeches, **BEN JONSON** *and* **JOHN MARSTON** *enter, haggard, breathing heavily.)*

WILL. Ben, Jack, why such dark brows? Stop and have some drink.

BEN. Let us first catch our breath.

MARSTON. It is all a matter of –

BEN. Don't talk. For God's sake, don't talk. Just fetch me a pot of ale.

SIR JOHN. Francis?

(Offstage: "Anon, anon, sir!")

WILL. You are not implicated in this Gunpowder affair?

BEN. Nothing so grand. We are in trouble over being writers.

MARSTON. How did I let you persuade me to help generate this theatrical artifact?

BEN. You cowardly bum fuck, you begged me to put your name on the project. You even tried to convince me to get rid of Chapman.

MARSTON. Well, then, since that unfortunate man is already in confinement, why don't we lay the blame on him for the aberrant speeches?

BEN. Because you wrote them, arse blight.

MARSTON. Yes, but it is Chapman who is incarcerated in the Tower. Why incriminate ourselves as well?

BEN. Do you know that this man aspires to be a clergyman? If God forbid he should ever achieve that sanctified state, I prophesy he will be hanged by his own clerical collar.

MARSTON. I was merely trying to purge the snottery of our slimy time…

BEN. There you go again.

MARSTON. ...and preserve the particulars of my personal honor.

BEN. You have deposited what is left of your personal honor in the privy.

SIR JOHN. Will you please tell us what is at stake here?

BEN. You know that Marston, Chapman and I were commissioned to write a play together.

WILL. Yes, I saw it performed at Blackfriars. *Eastward Ho!*

BEN. Well, this scurrilous foul mouth in his infinite wisdom thought it might be appropriate to take some satirical swipes at the Scots.

SIR JOHN. Is he mad?

MARSTON. It was excogitated with the best intentionality.

WILL. I was uneasy about those lines when I heard them spoken from the stage. They were bound to offend the King.

BEN. Which is exactly what befell us. Some busybody informed our Scottish monarch that his countrymen were being vilified and his land of birth impugned. He thereupon wrote out warrants for the three of us.

SIR JOHN. And Chapman was arrested?

BEN. No, he turned himself in.

SIR JOHN. I advise you both to do the same.

BEN. Jack can expect no more than a month or two in Newgate. It is a third offense for me. I can already feel the lash upon my backbone and the screws tightening on my knuckles. Last time, they branded me on the thumb. This time, they will cut them both off. Along with my stones.

WILL. I will speak for you.

SIR JOHN. You had better sober up first.

BEN. And what would your testimony accomplish, you bibulous poet.

WILL. I think I have some influence with the King. I have just delivered him my Scottish play. *(bitter)* Having joined his circle of flatterers.

SIR JOHN. He is very sensitive about the Scots, and sniffs conspiracy everywhere. Take care this mistrustful mastiff doesn't bite you on the rump as well.

WILL. I have not offended him and I believe my play will please him.

SIR JOHN. So long as you have included some diabolical witches, eh?

MARSTON. Masquerading as demonic bitches.

BEN. Don't talk!

(WILL *walks out of his room into a scene with* JAMES, *King of Great Britain.* JAMES *is sleeping on his throne.* WILL *goes offstage and gives a harrumph which wakes him.*)

JAMES. Welcome, Master Shakespeare. I have read your *Macbeth*. We have much to speak about.

WILL. Sire, I feel deeply honored to have had the opportunity to pay you…

JAMES. Yes, yes.

WILL. …service.

JAMES. Well, I must confess, you have done us Stuarts proud. This play is a great historical testimony to our Scottish past and our English future. Eight kings! And all of them Scotsmen!

WILL. Thank you, Your Majesty.

JAMES. It is also a testimony to our present, by which I mean your treatment of the witches, and your allusion to the Gunpowder plot.

WILL. I am happy you noticed that, your Majesty.

JAMES. Your Porter is especially on the mark. *(reading)* "Faith, here's an equivocator, who could swear in both the scales against either scale; who committed treason enough, for God's sake, yet could not equivocate to heaven. O, come in, equivocator."

WILL. You read those lines like an accomplished actor.

JAMES. You were thinking there of the late Father Garnet, no?

WILL. Of the kind of clerical evasion he represented, yes. "The equivocation of the fiend that lies like truth."

JAMES. Better and better. "Lies like truth" is a good way of describing the quality of heresy…

WILL. Or the nature of art.

JAMES. Yes, that's good. Indeed, sir.

WILL. And did the rest of my tragedy please you, too?

JAMES. Passing well. I particularly liked the Witch's line *(clears his throat to orate)* "Her husband's to Aleppo gone, master o' the Tiger:/But in a sieve I'll thither sail,/And, like a rat without a tail,/I'll do and I'll do and I'll do." Wasn't that a reference to Agnes Thompson, who threatened to sink the vessel of my Queen?

WILL. It was, your Majesty. You have been an invaluable source of inspiration to me in the writing of the play.

JAMES. You flatter me.

WILL. A lowly commoner cannot flatter a great king.

JAMES. Shakespeare –

WILL. Yes, your Majesty?

JAMES. There are even more similarities between your play and the recent conspiracy.

WILL. *(startled)* How so, your Majesty?

JAMES. Well, most obviously, both revolve around a plot to kill a beloved monarch, and both bring the villains to justice with miraculous historical consequences. I thought you very shrewd in the way you validated the Stuarts' right to the Scottish throne.

WILL. Thank you, your Majesty. *(Pause)* Your Majesty –

JAMES. And the way you had the ghost of Banquo empty the room. "The table's full." Ho, ho.

WILL. Thank you, you Majesty. May I–?

JAMES. Yes?

WILL. Do I have your gracious leave to beg a favor?

JAMES. You do.

WILL. May I speak for Ben Jonson?

JAMES. *(stiffening)* Jonson!

WILL. A fellow playwright and a long-time comrade.

JAMES. And a vile calumniator of the Scottish people.

WILL. I have reason to believe he was not the author of those offending lines in *Eastward Ho.*

JAMES. How do you know that?

WILL. There were three collaborators on the play.

JAMES. Then all three share responsibility.

WILL. Sire, you have just experienced a miraculous escape through the personal intervention of our blessed Lord. The people are celebrating your deliverance with bonfires. Is this a time to punish some poor playwright for a few careless errors?

JAMES. Go on.

WILL. I know Ben Jonson to be very partial to the Scottish people. He visits Edinburgh every Easter season. He is a good friend of your Scottish countryman, John Drummond of Hawthornden, and has tutored his young son William with his verses.

JAMES. Libel must be punished.

WILL. Perhaps a few nights in the Tower?

JAMES. What?

WILL. On bread and water? He would sorely miss his ale.

JAMES. Master Shakespeare, this is not your business.

WILL. *(dejected)* No, my liege. I have exceeded my...

JAMES. Tell your friend Ben Jonson to submit himself to the constabulary. Perhaps another trip to Scotland–on foot–would be a fitting punishment.

WILL. And a pardon. **(JAMES** *nods)*

WILL. Marston and Chapman, too?

JAMES. Marston and Chapman, too.

WILL. I am dizzy with gratitude.

JAMES. Then in that delirious state you have my leave to stumble home.

(**SHAKESPEARE** *leaves the room, bowing backwards as the King turns once more to read his play.*)

(**WILL** *staggers over to his room in Cripplegate. Lights on* **WILL** *washing his face and hands over and over.*)

BEN. *(bursting in, carrying some papers)* How went your meeting with the King?

WILL. You and Marston will be pardoned.

BEN. Thank God.

WILL. I feel stained.

BEN. By begging the King for our pardon?

WILL. No, by writing a play for him.

BEN. I've read your *Macbeth*. It is a mighty achievement.

WILL. It validates a worthless tyrant's right to the throne.

BEN. Do you think that in three hundred years, anyone will give a billy goat's belch over why you had written it?

WILL. You are not repelled by my fawning behavior?

BEN. It is a fawning world. How else would food appear on your table? Through magic? Far from being repelled by the reasons you wrote this Scottish play, I am exhilarated by the results. It is a great work of art, a superb chronicle of an ambitious man's descent into hell.

WILL. Do you speak of its hero or its author?

BEN. What!?

WILL. I have joined that man in hell. Macbeth says he has murdered sleep. He has certainly murdered mine, along with my tranquility, my confidence, my peace. I waver between painful insomnia and horrid dreams of assassins, witches, and savage man-eating horses.

BEN. Compose nothing but masques or satires like these in my hand, and your nights will pass undisturbed. Sleeplessness is the price one pays for genius. Life may be short, as the Greek physician Hippocrates has said, but art is long. *(He drops the papers on* **WILL**'s *desk.)*

WILL. Quote Hippocrates to me when I am rotting in cold obstruction, my throat clogged with clay, my liver gnawed by earthworms.

BEN. Do not lose your love of literature.

WILL. I still love literature, Ben, it is humanity that troubles me. When you first chased Marston into this room, he said he was in "mortal terror." I have since understood what that meant: terror of mortals, fear of mankind.

BEN. Lord, what ghouls these mortals be, eh?

WILL. Thou hast said it. Myself included.

BEN. No, Will. Terror is an accessory of mortality. But were each of us created in your image, ah, things would be so different.

WILL. Ben, you are a great flatterer.

BEN. Not so, my William Shakespeare, my sweet Will. You are the very best of us, a liberal wit tempered by a gentle, modest soul.

WILL. I am blushing either from excessive drink or excessive blarney. Do your commendations come from conviction or compassion?

BEN. From the heart, Will. From the heart.

WILL. And not from pity for my diminishing faith in mankind?

BEN. Pity is one of the purgative elements of tragedy.

WILL. And terror is the other, which is why I have finished with the form.

BEN. Finished with tragedy? What, no more *Hamlets*, no more *Lears*, no more Scottish plays?

WILL. No more tales of terror that leave us looking into the abyss.

BEN. You will be left with precious little to write about.

WILL. I could write a masque or two for the Queen.

BEN. That would make her very happy. She loves your work, she tells me, and seems hardly impervious to your charms as well.

WILL. Did you know she visited me lately in these lodgings in male attire?

BEN. Like Rosalind in *As You Like It?*

WILL. In doublet and hose.

BEN. Which you removed to have her as *you* like it?

WILL. That could never happen.

BEN. Why not? If a cat can look at a King, a literary lion can ogle a Queen.

WILL. Yes, and have his eyes plucked out for his pains.

BEN. No worry, Will. Every genius is allowed a certain degree of poetic licentiousness.

(**WILL** *shrugs.*)

BEN. And now, dear Will, I will leave you to sketch out your next play. You have written only one thus far this year, and your annual quota is two.

(*A knock on the door. It is* **QUEEN ANNE** *again disguised as a boy.*)

BEN. Ah, what lad is this entering upon the sacred grove of Arden? No introductions, please. There is no time. Will, goodbye. And goodbye to you, young man. May you find tongues in trees and sermons in stones (*he indicates this is a pun on testicles, then leaves*).

WILL. I am happy to see your Majesty.

ANNE. I am happy to see you. But I do fear Jonson recognized me. Will he be secret?

WILL. He is in trouble enough at present with your husband.

ANNE. And so indeed am I.

WILL. Can I do anything to help?

ANNE. I know not. I was hoping–

(*sounds upon the stairs*)

WILL. Someone else is coming. Into my cupboard. Quickly.

(**QUEEN ANNE** *goes into the cupboard.* **SIR JOHN** *arrives. He is a little drunk.*)

WILL. It is very early in the morning, Sir John.

SIR JOHN. No, it is very late at night!

WILL. This is not the most convenient time to visit. Why have you come?

SIR JOHN. I had hoped to take a nap here and sober up. I have just come from the debauch of my life.

WILL. You must go home. *(SIR JOHN looks crestfallen; WILL takes pity.)*

SIR JOHN. You can't spare me a moment to rest my drunken bones?

WILL. A moment only. What was the occasion?

SIR JOHN. *(warming up)* A feast at the palace followed by a masque.

WILL. The King was there?

SIR JOHN. *(nodding)* Blind drunk. During the prologue, his Majesty got up to dance with the Queen of Sheba, but fell down flat upon his face, and was carried to an inner chamber. There he was laid on a bed of state, which was not a little defiled by the belly juices Sheba had just bestowed upon his garments.

WILL. Thank God the Queen was not present to witness this.

SIR JOHN. I have seen her in a like condition, disgorging her dinner in a neighboring room.

WILL. I know her as a woman temperate and virtuous.

SIR JOHN. Virtuous, say you? The mistress of Robert Catesby, majordomo of the Gunpowder Plot?

WILL. I do not believe she was privy to that affair.

SIR JOHN. I'd bet my knighthood she was, even if I cannot prove it.

(He starts to heave.)

WILL. Sir John, I think you'd best find your way home before you bestow your Gaelic dinner over my Persian carpet.

SIR JOHN. Thank you, Will. *(Handkerchief to his mouth, he exits.)* Farewell.

(**QUEEN ANNE** *emerges from* **WILL***'s cupboard offstage.*)

ANNE. Will.

WILL. I know I have no right to ask the truth of this.

ANNE. There is some truth in it, Will, a morsel, but –

WILL. I will only comment on how the court of James, *your* court, has managed to debauch even that good old knight John Harington.

ANNE. It is true that Catesby had been my lover. It is true that I consented to the deposition of the King. But I never agreed to the murder of innocent people.

WILL. *(takes her hands in his, and looks)* Yet, here's a spot.

ANNE. Where?

WILL. In my imagination.

ANNE. *(rubbing her hands)* I was desperate to escape this hateful marriage. I could think of no other way.

WILL. No other way than bloodshed?

ANNE. Catesby spoke only of exile.

WILL. And you believed him.

ANNE. I wanted to believe him.

WILL. You never thought that others might be sacrificed to his ends?

ANNE. *(crying)* Somewhere I must have known it.

WILL. Or of the terrible vengeance the King would inflict after the plot had failed?

ANNE. I was thinking only of myself and my children.

WILL. Blood will have blood, they say.

ANNE. *(recovering herself and wiping her eyes)* Will, if all you are going to do is quote from your work, then our relationship is over. I can just as soon go home and read the plays.

WILL. Actually, our friendship as you call it, never really got started.

ANNE. Too true.

WILL. What will you do now?

ANNE. I will return to my detested husband, God help me, and beg his forgiveness.

WILL. And I will return to Stratford. There is much to be mended in my marriage. And my daughters need me.

ANNE. And so farewell, Will Shakespeare. *(She turns to go.)*

WILL. You are a gallant and spirited woman for whom I have the deepest respect.

ANNE. Do you still respect me, Will? *(WILL nods.)* Then I have no regrets. *(She kisses him gently on the lips and leaves.)*

(WILL returns to his desk and writes, reading as he does:)

Tired with all these, for restful death I cry,
As to behold desert a beggar born,
And needy nothing trimm'd in jollity,
And purest faith unhappily forsworn,
And gilded honour shamefully misplac'd,
And maiden virtue rudely strumpeted,
And right perfection wrongfully disgrac'd,
And strength by limping sway disabled
And art made tongue-tied by authority,
And folly, doctor-like, controlling skill,
And simple truth miscall'd simplicity,
And captive good attending captain ill....

(BEN JONSON has entered during WILL's reading and listens quietly, interrupting before the final couplet.)

BEN. A sonnet, Will? Inspired by your outcast state?

WILL. You again.

BEN. Forgive the intrusion. I left my new Masque behind. *(gathering them up)* You haven't composed a fourteen liner since your patron Southampton was locked up in the Tower.

WILL. As usual, you remember more about my writing than I do.

BEN. How else would my poor verses ever hope to compete? And now you're composing another piece of poesy on the abuses of authority. What are you planning?

WILL. A return to Stratford, where I intend to reflect on the question, why I write.

BEN. Ah, so it's no longer a matter of holding a mirror up to nature?

WILL. That will always be my ultimate purpose. But I was wondering if, as Sir John believes, there might not be a more active motive for writing than reflecting things as they are.

BEN. Active? You? A poor player, strutting and fretting his hour upon the stage?

WILL. It may be time for this poor player to find a higher purpose.

BEN. You realize you are abandoning the London stage to me?

WILL. For a time. I hope to return before too long with new weapons and in new armor.

BEN. Well, thanks to the pardon you squeezed out from the King, I fully intend to exploit your rash decision. I am done with masques. I too am planning some major statement, through a series of immortal comical satires.

WILL. England's stage will be the richer for it.

BEN. *(moved)* So this is goodbye. For once, I know not what to say. Yes, I do. When I outlive you, your funeral obsequies will include a fulsome Jonsonian ode to the memory of our beloved author and what he has left us. No other poet will ever receive such tribute from my hands.

WILL. Goodbye, Ben. If you need a writing space for the next few months, you are welcome to my rooms. I would be happier living in Stratford knowing that good poetry is being composed in Cripplegate.

BEN. Come here! *(He enfolds WILL in a strong bear hug.)*

WILL. Oh rare Ben Jonson, dearest of friends.

    (**BEN** *is too moved to speak.* **WILL** *picks up a bag and leaves.*)

BEN. *(writing the first lines of* Volpone *at* **WILL***'s desk)* "Good morning to the day and next my gold. Open the shrine that I may see my saint."

    (**JOHN MARSTON** *peeks his head around the door.*)

MARSTON. The magnificate William Shakespeare is not approachable at this temporal moment?

BEN. No, you bombastic, turgidious, lubrical, defunctive knave, he is not approachable at this temporal moment. What in the name of all your pitiful assaults on the tortured English tongue do you wish now from William Shakespeare?

MARSTON. I have materialized in these chambers to articulate to him my strenuous gratification for accomplishing the king's exoneration.

BEN. *(going after the wash basin again)* I think this occasion calls for another purge. *(He grabs the wash basin and chases* **MARSTON** *down the stairs.)*

MARSTON. *(in the distance shouting)* Mortal terror!!!!

Curtain